For Jon-Jo with love
M.I.

First published 1989 by
Walker Books Ltd, 87 Vauxhall Walk
London SE11 5HJ

© 1989 Mick Inkpen

First printed 1989
Printed and bound by L.E.G.O., Vicenza, Italy

British Library Cataloguing in Publication Data
Inkpen, Mick
Jojo's revenge.
I. Title
823′.914 [J]

ISBN 0-7445-1235-2

Jojo's Revenge!

Written and illustrated by
MICK INKPEN

WALKER BOOKS
LONDON

Like all babies Jojo
was squeezed and
squashed and passed
around a lot.
Like pass the parcel.

Everyone wanted to prod him to make him smile. Or poke their fingers into his mouth to see if he had grown any teeth.

People would knit him
cardigans that were
too big.
Or too small.
The silliest one had a
matching pom-pom hat
with ear flaps.

And though his cot was full of furry animals, the things he really wanted were always out of reach.

At night, just as Jojo was beginning to enjoy a good yell, someone would always find a way to stop him.

And once, even
his mum got cross
with him for filling
his nappy.
"Oh Jojo," she said,
"not now!"

So one day, to get his own back, Jojo decided that instead of eating his dinner, he would wear it!

After this there was
no stopping him.
Every day Jojo managed
to try on his breakfast,
his dinner or his tea.
"It's because he's like
me," said Grandpa.
"He's artistic!"

Jojo's mum bought
him some face
paints to play with.
But Jojo ignored them.
He preferred to paint
with porridge.

Then one day Jojo's mum went out, leaving his grandpa to look after him. "Try not to let him make too much mess with his dinner," she said.

When she got back she was amazed. Jojo's plate was empty and there was not a single scrap of food on him.
"Grandpa! How did you do it?" she said.

"Like this!"
said Jojo's grandpa.